# This Stage
## of Life
### - Self-Discovery -

JASMINE SAMUEL

# Dedication

This book is dedicated to everyone who has ever felt that they lost their way in the journey of life and are fighting their way back to find themselves again.

# CONTENTS

# ACKNOWLEDGMENTS

Thank you to my editor for the patience you have had with me and the support you have given me. Without you I truly do not believe I would have made it to this point, you made my dream a reality.

Thank you to my family for always showing me the fun and crazy side of life. When we are together, we can only make happy memories.

Thank you to my dog, Thor, and my cat, Estrella, for keeping me company every time I write.

I want to give my highest thanks to God for supporting and loving me through it all.

To my mom and dad, thank you for supporting me on this journey even though you had no idea it was happening. You both have always shown me how to be an independent woman and to always have love and kindness in my heart. I would not be the person I am today without you both.

Mom, you have done so much for me that I can never repay you, but I will continue every day to try and show you how much you mean to me. I feel proud to say that I am just like you. You are a strong beautiful woman and your unconditional love is what drives me to be the best I can be in life.

Dad, you have taught me more life lessons than I can count and I continue to use it every day. There are countless moments in my life where I catch myself saying "My dad told me..." or "My dad does it like this..." You have done so much and you deserve to rest and we deserve to make more memories together. I love you like a fresh vegetable.

And to a very special person in my life, you have been my motivation through it all. You have kept me sane, taught me to love myself before others, and have shown me that there is more meaning to life. I owe so much to your love and support you gave me. Thank you for giving me a new home and diversifying my life. You will always hold a very special spot in my heart.

# *My Songbird* I

My songbird has left me for the day. I watch her stretch her wings, then do a little hop off the perch before soaring into the sky out of my line of sight. I hop off my day bed, trying to mimic her graceful qualities to go downstairs. The savory aroma from the kitchen had drifted itself through the empty hallways and box filled rooms to meet my nose hairs. I half-walk, half-skip my way into the kitchen to find my topless, basketball shorts-wearing fiancé stirring ingredients in a pot on the stove.

"I'm surprised you found the cooking ware in all of these boxes."

I squeeze his waist, hugging him from behind then placed my lips on the stubble of his cheek.

"I'm surprised you still haven't unpacked anything yet."

He gave me a stern gaze, but returned my caress with a kiss of his own and a spoonful of food to taste for flavor. I add a dash of my favorite seasoning and give him my approval, signifying the meal was ready to be devoured.

"I'm waiting on you to help me."

I open the cabinet to reach for the only pair of bowls in the empty shelves. He had placed them on the third shelf and it was too high for me to reach. Like a hero, he swooped in to retrieve the bowls for me.

"Baby, I'm working all day. I'd like to come back to a home at the end of the day, not a house full of boxes." He placed the bowls in my hands, wrapped his hand around mine and stared deeply into my eyes. "I want the best for us."

I looked down at our warm cocoa fingers wrapped together.

"Okay Mister *Associate Director*. I'll start unpacking tomorrow," I grinned and cupped my hand on his cheek before moving to the stove to dish out our dinner.

I was proud of my man. He had worked odd jobs here and there to support me through college until he eventually landed a marketing job with the big boys across town. After four years of commitment and hard work, he was promoted to one of the top positions in his company. I no longer had to teach anymore during the summer at the middle school where I work. Since then, our lives had been a dream. He proposed the night after his promotion at our favorite lakeside restaurant. Then, three months later, we purchased our first home across town in a gated community. Still, I had the biggest surprise yet that I was exploding to share with him, but I was waiting for the perfect moment.

We made our way to the dining room where we sat on our shiny, hardwood floor to eat our dinner. The boxes surrounding us were our only view. Our new mahogany table will be delivered this weekend. At least then, we would be eye level to the window.

"Did your songbird come back today?" he broke our silence, speaking between bites.

"Yes," I nodded. "Every day since we've moved in."

The blue and red bird had appeared the first day we moved in. My fiancé was whistling as we brought boxes in the house from our rented moving truck when the bird landed on the banister of our porch to listen to his song. The songbird stayed with us all day as my fiancé whistled and I tossed it crumbs from our snacks. Since then, it has come back every day, singing its song and awaiting treats. We bought it a perch with special bird seed to sit and sing in front of our bedroom window. Every now and then, when my fiancé sees it, they share a tune together and I toss it extra treats.

The night ended briefly as we began to prepare for bed. In bed, we snuggle close together, my head on his heart and his arms wrapped around my side. The bed feels warm and full of love as he kisses my forehead and whispers to me, "I feel something big is going to happen tomorrow."

"I hope so." I whisper back.

"Good night, I love you."

"I love you."

That night replays in my head every day, but that night was eight months ago.

The next day, he woke up in a hurry to make it in time for an early work meeting. He had slept through his first two alarms and was rushing through the house trying to find his clothes in boxes to make it in time. I felt a quick peck in my sleep, but then he was gone before I could wake up to say goodbye.

Less than five miles down the road, he was stopped by a policeman for speeding eight miles over the speed limit through our neighborhood. Seven minutes into the encounter, the powerful bang of the Glock 22 echoed through the streets and he was taken from me, in broad daylight, on an early Wednesday morning, with no witnesses and only five miles from home - from me.

They said you had a bad attitude and reached for a weapon, which was never found. They said you posed a threat and the officer acted in self-defense. They said you had a criminal record and a history of violence. But I know you and I know what happened.

I know that you were targeted for the rich melanin in your skin. I know you were annoyed by the third traffic stop in two weeks for being a brother in this type of neighborhood. I know you were reaching for the mail in your console which proved you lived in this neighborhood since the last police officer had not believed you since we had not yet changed our address on our licenses. I know they feared you for your dark chocolate skin, broad shoulders and tattoos. I know the boy who stole snacks from the corner store at seventeen and who was in those high school fights was not the same man they encountered that day. I know you for who you really are, not who they demonized to make your murder seem justified, as if they were upholding the law and defending their right to the second amendment.

I rub my enlarged belly as I lay in front of my window for the songbird who has not returned since your passing. I feel a kick beneath my hand as a tear rolls down my cheek. No matter how much I whistle and toss crumbs, it never returns and neither will you.

# Who Am I?

I say my name loud and proud for everyone to know.

I am not scared, timid, nor embarrassed of my name.

If you know me, then you know my name is my statement.

All four names stand bold on its own, but together they are powerful.

But who am I?

Take away my parents, I am an orphan.

Take away my family, friends, and lover, I am a loner.

Take away my career, I am unemployed.

Take away my possessions, I am humbled.

Am I just what I have and who I know?

Without these things am I unable to grow?

What makes a person who they are and who they are not?

I am who I am because of my name.

My name is my entity, my individual mark in this world.

The moment I was born I was looked at and labeled.

One possession I take through life that I am in control of.

I can add to it, take away or even replace it how I please.

My name is my honor which speaks my past, present, and future.

I wear it proud through it all.

No fear, shame, nor humbleness.

Because through it all it has stayed glued to me.

So, I thank all that I am and all that I have.

Thank you to my parents for setting my stage and delivering my name.

Thank you to my family, friends, and lover for letting my name be heard.

Thank you to my job for adding wealth to my name.

Thank you to my possessions for adding value to my name.

And thank you God for being with me since before I had a name.

So, who am I?

I am the image of my name.

# When the Roles Reverse

I try to be okay with what you are doing.

I want to be fair and give you time with your boys like when I go out with my girls.

I tell myself that it is your turn now to enjoy the night without me, just as I have done before.

I left without telling you, stayed out until the sun came up and drank until I could walk no more.

Now it is your turn and all I can do is worry.

Are you safe?

Are any girls trying to get with you?

Are you around good people?

Are you able to come back home?

The tears swell in my eyes as my anxiety takes over and only the worst possibilities come to mind.

I wonder when did my trust begin to fade?

But is it you who I fail to trust,

Or the outside world?

I have had enough time in the streets to know what goes on.

But who do I blame, but myself?

When I am the one who asked for freedom and gave you yours?

# Alone

Hello, love.

It has been a while since we've last spoken.

I miss being your friend and I am ready to return if you are.

You look different, seem different, act different.

I am glad you've grown and matured, but there is a change within you that does not belong.

Are you tired?

You look tired.

The bags under your eyes and sag in your cheeks show me that you are tired.

The countless thoughts and worries are flooding your mind, keeping you awake at night and waking you up early.

Are you stressed?

You seem stressed.

Trying to live up to the expectations of others and, mostly, yourself.

Trying to please everyone and make them happy, but forgetting about your own happiness.

Are you lost?

You act lost.

Your insecurities are clouding your judgment, making you second guess every choice you make and everything you say.

Unsure where your path lies and seeking advice from the world.

But I am here now,

To bring positivity to your mind and to calm your thoughts,

To reassure you that you are enough just as you are and you deserve happiness,

To trust yourself and to follow your intuition, for God has already given you all that you need.

Are you ready for me?

I am ready for you.

I too have been incomplete without you,

Seeking more to life that I do not have,

Trying to understand my part in this world, hoping and praying for better.

We need each other,

For I am you and you are me and together,

We are not alone.

# At My Intersection

At my intersection I play the game of I spy.

I spy the cars driving by,

On the four-lane avenue divided in half by the trees, shrubs and flowers.

Every now and then I spy people within these cars.

I spy through their tinted windows as I wonder if the people inside can see as little of me as I see of them.

I spy a hand and an arm dangling effortlessly out a window with their music bumping.

I spy hair, flying in the wind as the breeze blows by.

I spy a head bob forward and backward, up and down as the truck plunges into the dip in the road.

At times, when these cars turn down my drive, I spy a face,

# This Stage of Life - Self Discovery

Sometimes watching me as I watch it.

I spy the people passing by.

The family of four who live down the road. They all ride bikes.

The bald man who walks his dog every day, but crosses the street when he reaches my home.

I spy the couple across the way sitting on their porch behind laptops and a pink "Queer" flag that blows in the wind, blocking my view.

I spy the emergency vehicles zooming by,

Some with their sirens and lights on ready to serve and protect,

Making the dogs howl and me wonder,

What happened?

Where are they going?

Is someone I know in trouble?

But sometimes, when the road is clear,

And the plants and animals are still,

I spy myself watching life before me, so interested in others.

My eyes bounce as the multitude of thoughts begin to flood my mind,

Waiting, hoping, wishing for the road to get busy again to distract me.

As the time passes and the stillness continues, my heart beats a little faster and my breath becomes shallower.

I close my eyes and take a deep breath.

The sun shining light into the darkness under my eyelids,

And then, I see it,

A brief glance at my dreams, but enough to make me see clearly.

I open my eyes and get up to move beyond my intersection,

Because I no longer want to play the game of I spy.

Now,

I live my own life.

# What I Really Want

I want to smell the cologne on your body as I pull your shirt over your head.

I want to watch your smile vanish as you lower your head to kiss my figure ever so gently.

I want to feel the shiver across my skin as your tongue traces your favorite parts of my body.

I want to release my control into your firm, but gentle hands as you hold me like your most prized possession.

I want to disappear from this world into the music of your heartbeat as I lay on your chest.

I want to hear the longing in your voice as you whisper your desires in my ear.

I want to experience the contrast as our rough and smooth body parts meet.

I want to see the smile on your face as we look each other in the eyes.

I want to lay in your strong, protecting arms, shielding me from all of my worries and fears.

Now, since you always ask me,

"What is it that you really want?"

I have told you and you can give it to me.

I want you.

# Take Me Back in Time

Someone please give me a time machine,

So I can go back in time and right my wrongs.

I promise it will only be for one night,

To prevent what happened a couple of nights ago.

I know, I know,

Do not regret, for every mistake is a lesson learned,

But I promised that I have already learned this lesson before.

I just want to go back in spirit just to talk with myself,

Whisper a few words to be my voice of reason,

Uncluttering the thoughts in my mind to take control of my emotions.

I would separate myself until I could be me again, without the rage,

And tell myself that I can't control the situation, but I can control myself.

I would speak only what I really felt and not what was led by hurt.

Someone please give me a time machine,

So maybe you would still be here.

# *My Songbird* II

"I can't do this anymore! Make it stop!" I screamed at the room full of people watching me, all waiting for the same surprise.

The tears and sweat that rolled down my face felt like sizzling hot grease on a lit stove. I looked around the room waiting for anyone to save me from the anguish of childbirth, but no one did. Instead, they just kept watching me as if I was a zoo animal fighting to get out of the cage, which is exactly what I felt like at this moment.

A few nurses sputtered words of encouragement whilst also trying to do their jobs, saying things like, "You can do this. You've already come so far. Just a little more," as if all I needed at this moment was a little motivation. I scoffed at them all. Their words were drowned out by my screaming. Of course, the effects of labor and delivery were the main cause of my pain, but a part of me was finally releasing the one emotion I had pent up since the day of your death.

Anger.

Somewhere along the way I had skipped this part of the grieving process and it was coming in full force now. I think back to the day of your funeral, the same day a certain member of my family decided to share the news of my pregnancy to, in their words, "lighten the mood." I became surrounded by people unsure of whether to send their condolences or congratulate me first. I had searched through the crowd to find the snitch who exposed my secret so I could tell them off, but I was engulfed in the crowd of pity and soon, that was the only emotion I felt.

But now, the pain and the screams released the anger that had built up for nine months and it did not want to be withheld any longer. My eyes closed as I blocked out the faces, voices and beeping monitors around me. I focused on my anger instead of what was about to slide out from between my legs. Every curse word that I ever learned came flying out of my mouth. I am angry and I deserve to be heard.

I am angry at the man who pulled the trigger, a murderer hiding behind a badge and uniform. I am angry at the entire Department of Justice for having a name so powerful and trustworthy, but only providing inequality and unanswered questions. It took three long months for the footage to be released and only then were we able to know what really happened that day.

You were pulled over at the intersection where the big pine tree shadows half of the block. You rolled your window down with your documents already in your hand. You spoke first, "Sorry man. I know I was going a little fast back there, but I am in a hurry to get to work. I will slow down from here and I'll take the ticket, but I really need to head on." You flashed your award-worthy smile and handed the documents to the man who would become your murderer.

He did not even acknowledge you. He just snatched the documents out of your hands and replied, "Where do you work?"

You responded and the man chuckled, "Yeah, right. Just wait right here." Five minutes later he returned to your window and asked you to step out of the car so he could search you.

"Why do you need to search me?"

"Your address is about thirty minutes away from this neighborhood and we've had a few thefts recently. It's standard precaution," he lied.

You rolled your eyes. You knew your rights and you were not going to allow him search you without reasonable cause. "My fiancé and I just moved here a few weeks ago. This weekend, we're going to get our addresses changed on our IDs. Look, I have proof of residency right here–."

"Sir!" The officer yelled at you and the camera shuffled. Your eyes dropped to his right side and grew wide. I could tell that he had his hand on his gun holster. "Keep your hands where I can see them! Step out of the vehicle now!"

Your body tensed and you moved in slow-motion to return your hands to the steering wheel. "Alright man, let's just calm down. I'm coming out, but I'll feel more comfortable if I have my fiancé on the phone," your voice trembled as if you were choosing your words very carefully. "You can see my hands sir. I'm just going to pick up my phone and–"

BANG!

I jumped the first time I saw the video. My eyes closed tightly like they are now to avoid seeing what I heard.

I am angry at the police department who made countless excuses to justify your murder. He was a relatively new officer, only two years on the field, but already near his mid-thirties. I am angry at his wife, who delivered a fruit basket and a note saying, "I'm sorry for what my husband did," on the day of your funeral, which I threw away and burned.

"Sweetie, you need to push."

One of the nurses squeezed my arm lightly and I swatted her away,

"No!" I screamed at her, never opening my eyes. The darkness was comfort to my anger.

"Mother and baby's heart rate is increasing rapidly," another nurse said.

Soon, multiple voices began speaking at once. I blocked them out and focused on my anger.

I am angry at my family and yours for treating me like a patient on suicide watch. Constant surveillance and cautious words so that I would not get worked up and excite the baby. I was never given the time to grieve on my own. Even with all of their monitoring, my blood pressure was consistently high at every doctor visit.

The media visited our home multiple times for a statement from me to support their hashtags with your name, but each time they were turned away by the same family who kept me locked in the house for my own safety, or so they say.

But most of all, I was angry with myself. Angry that I could not be by your side in your last moments of life. Angry that I had not unpacked the boxes sooner so you could have saved time that morning or even woken you up when I heard your first alarm. Angry that I never told you the big surprise that was growing in my uterus. I failed at being a wife to you and taking care of you how I was supposed to.

I tried to take a deep breath, but my breath had become shallower and my hands began to tremble. The pain from my lower body had traveled upward causing my head to throb torturously and I screamed again.

"Get us to the OR room now!" was the last thing I heard, then everything was silent.

Dark and silent.

I felt nothing.

# To My Future Child

I have yet to meet you, but I know that you are beautiful, kind, generous, funny, handsome, loving, spiritual, talented and gifted.

I want you to know that this world is yours and experience as much of it as you can.

Your life will not be easy, no matter how much we give to you,

But make the best of each moment and know that you are never alone.

Express yourself for all that you are without fear nor shame.

You are a flower who grows from your roots, so remember who you are,

And if you are neglected, your petals will begin to fall, leaving you barren and unrecognizable.

I will show you what is right and what is wrong and guide you through this thing called life.

You are kind and loving and it is easy to share your heart with others,

But know your value and know your worth is too great that some people do not deserve you.

Yes, even those you love,

So choose wisely on the people in your life.

Those who deserve you are those who add more value to your worth.

You deserve to receive just as much as you give.

Do not be afraid to put yourself first, you are your own greatest fan.

The same way you love and care for others, you must love and care for yourself.

I am sorry to say that there will be dark days,

Days full of sadness, hurt, and despair.

And there is nothing I can do or say to prevent this from happening,

But accept support from your loved ones around you who have also experienced these days,

And be strong to make it to the better days,

Days full of love, laughter, and joy.

Remember that you are never alone.

I will try to reduce your pain as much as I can,

But even if I am not there and your friends and family are not near,

Look inside yourself for the King, always remember that God lives within.

I love you, I am proud of you, and I will cherish every moment we spend together, both good and bad.

Right now, I am not where I need to be in life to give to you,

So until the day we meet, I will prepare for you.

# On To Better Days

I have a vision of better days,

Where the skies are blue and the water turquoise.

Rainy days are followed by rainbows,

And every night is illuminated by starlight,

Where I am free from stress and oppression and the stress of oppression.

Money does not define how good of a life I have,

But rather is an addition to my happiness which cannot be taken away.

I envision myself living the life I deserve.

Peace, love, and happiness that's all I crave,

With a little bit of drama every now and then to keep me humbled and appreciative of what I have.

Who says life cannot be this way?

Oh, the colonizers who took us away as their slaves to learn their Western ways.

Well, I will gladly go back, on a one-way flight to the good old days,

Back when times were simpler,

And before they put is in this maze.

But for now, I keep on

Working and searching for the life I deserve,

So that one day this vision will become a clear reality.

# This Place Called America

How can I have pride in a country where my people have worked so hard just to have basic human rights?

Enslaved, segregated, discriminated and abused,

Tested on like lab rats and left to die in cold blood.

America,

Where having a little more melanin in your skin threatens others and gets you threatened too,

And being anything but a white male gets you belittled,

Where mass murders continue to happen because the NRA has the final say,

And women have to fight for control of their own bodies to this day.

Nature is flooded with trash,

Animals are killed just for fun.

America,

Where I watch my brothers and sisters being killed by Klansmen in police uniforms,

And countless bodies without a home lay in the street at night.

This has become our normal in this country called America,

But it takes much more to be "great again" or so they say.

America, honor your people and we will honor your faith.

# What Makes You So Different?

We all experience life's struggles.

Some have experienced more than others.

Through life's journey we will all experience pain,

But what you do with your pain is what makes you who you are.

You look at others and idolize them, dreaming of reaching their level.

Your dreams feel so far away from reality.

You think that because of your circumstances it could never be.

You hate on others for what you see,

And try to uplift yourself with words of hate,

Saying things like they do not know your struggles and all that you have been through.

If they were in your position, they would not have all that they have,

But wait...Do you know their position?

Do you know what they have been through on the inside?

Or are you just a viewer from the outside?

Your worst enemy is yourself,

The constant self-doubt and excuses hold you down.

It makes your dreams seem so far and unclear and your present so negative and poor.

Words hold so much more value than what you can ever believe,

So next time you catch yourself putting yourself down,

Say these words,

"I can do anything I put my mind to."

Then, put your words to action and get to work on your dream.

Take it one step at a time and always make time for rest.

Remember that you are great, you deserve prosperity and you are blessed with the tools to succeed.

All that is left for you to do is believe.

Moral: You can have anything they have and more.

# I Hope This Works

Lord, please make this the last time.

My heart can't take anymore.

I am tired of empty apologies and broken promises,

And seeking revenge to even the score.

Maybe we are both fools,

Ignoring your signs of moving on,

But there is still something here.

The love is not all gone.

Maybe what we are going through now,

Is the lesson we both need,

To prepare ourselves for what will come.

I hope, I plead,

Lord, please make this be the last time.

We are ready to get rid of the toxic ways,

The petty arguments that left us in silence for days,

Happy memories surrounded with tears, screams, and open wounds.

It is time to heal and move on.

We have done our share together and as individuals.

If you are ready to end it all, I will appeal.

As long as we are able to put in the work and trust in You,

Guide us through the pain-filled past,

To make this last.

Lord, please make this be the last time.

# Let Me Grow

You have planted the seed to your fruit tree.

You placed me in the sun,

Gave me good soil, water and enough love to nourish the world.

You watched your seed grow,

Through each season I have gained and lost my leaves.

You have supported and provided for me through it all,

To help me grow into the beautiful fruit tree you knew I could be.

But now it is time.

My fruit is ripe and full of seeds,

Wanting to explore, experience and grow on their own,

But you keep picking away at me taking all of my fruit so I cannot expand my growth,

Then nourishing me again so I can grow more.

The cycle continues time and time again.

There is only so much you can provide to me.

One day you will have to leave your beautiful fruit tree alone,

To keep my own fruit and grow on my own in other places away from you.

You are loved and appreciated for all of your hard work.

Now sit back and watch your fruit tree grow.

Soon you will have a forest of trees with more than enough to provide for you.

It is time.

# *My Songbird* III

I have never experienced as much stillness as I am at this moment. Everywhere I look I see light surrounding me, a bright white light that could blind you if you stared in one place for too long pierced its way into my cornea. As I looked around and remembered my last memory, fear washed over me.

I can remember the nurses and doctors screaming codes and the room filling with faces I had never seen before. I had felt still and motionless, but everything felt so surreal, as if I was having an out of body experience. Then everything became peaceful. I could not hear nor see anymore and I felt... relaxed. My body stayed still like this for a few moments as I enjoyed the feeling of nothingness. But a faint cry had emerged from the silence, distracting me from my momentary peace and bringing me here.

Here. A place that was still unknown and feared by me, but I followed the sound of the cry. I kept walking though and every step I took landed me in the same place. I heard the cry and I had to know who it belonged to, but there was no end in sight beyond this light. The sudden realization that I could not escape made me lay down and accept my fate.

Just as I was closing my eyes and preparing for whatever was in store for me next, blurry images flooded my view and the cry grew louder. I saw a woman lying on her back in the hospital bed.

"Is this me?" I ask myself as I stare closely at the scene before me. The hospital room looked different than what I remember and the nurses and doctor were also unrecognizable.

The images stilled in front of me and became clearer as time passed. I realized that I was not the woman in the image, but this scene seemed oddly familiar to me. The woman shared similar features to mine. Her wide, flared nose and big brown eyes matching her brown skin reminded me of myself. She lay breathless as the newborn she had just delivered was placed upon her chest. A grateful smile came across her face as she kissed the baby's forehead and looked up to the man beside her.

"Is that–?" I pondered. "It can't be."

Confusion filled my head as I gained understanding of the scene I was witnessing. My eyes were glued to the younger versions of my mother and father experiencing the birth of their only child. The love in their eyes and smiles on their faces as they looked at the newborn version of me caused a warm sensation to fill my body, a sensation that I had never felt before. Before I could grasp my reality, the scene ended and I was placed in front of another set of moving images.

This time, the images did not become still and clear, but rather passed by in a blur. Shivers crept down my spine as I watched my life unfold before my eyes. From my very first word, first step and first love to my very last day of school, last prom and last moment with you. Every moment of my life was before me, but I felt heavier as I witnessed our love story and I fell in love with you all over again.

Our first meeting was at the airport where we were both waiting for our flights back home. I saw you watching me from the gates and somehow ease your way behind me to present your ticket. Unfortunately for you, our seats were far apart on the plane which made it difficult for you to start a conversation. I had not noticed you until a few hours later after we landed and you "accidentally" bumped into me as we searched for our luggage.

I watched in awe as you fumbled with your words, but you made me laugh. We continued our conversation until we reached the airport's exit where we went our separate ways, but not before exchanging numbers. The next few weeks were blissful as we spoke every day and went out every weekend. But our fun was short-lived once the semester began at my university and my schedule became less available to you.

That was when our problems had begun. The jealousy and limited contact were enough for us to drift apart but our time apart only made our love grow stronger. Thinking of you had become my favorite hobby. The moments we had spent together had only brought me joy and once we reconnected a few months later, I promised never to let you go again.

After that, almost every memory included you. You made even my darkest days seem bearable. You brought tears to my eyes the day you proposed to me. With you, I was able to accomplish all of my dreams. The scenes continued to pass by my eyes until the day of your death and my whole life changed. I tried to look away, but the light and images were everywhere. I closed my eyes instead, trying to remember the happier moments of our lives together, but it seemed the memories were slipping away.

"You are stronger than this," a voice boomed in the distance startling me. I opened my eyes to search for the voice's owner, but

I could see no one. The images had disappeared again and everything had returned to the same bright white light as when I arrived.

"Hello?" I questioned the open space.

"You shouldn't be here. It's not your time," the voice responded to me.

I thought back to my last memory in the hospital and the sustained beep of the monitor before I came into this stillness and I could only think of one explanation. "Are you God?"

The voice chuckled and a body emerged from the light. "If I were God, you wouldn't have to ask. You always knew how to make me laugh."

I paused in belief not believing my eyes. "It's you."

"It's me." He opened his arms wide and I ran to him. My heart pounded within me as we share our embrace. I wanted to stay in his arms and escape life with him in this place forever, but I felt his muscles relax and he pulled away.

"What are you doing here? You can't stay here." He stared into my eyes and I believed he was able to read exactly what I was thinking. I broke down in tears as I explained how my life has been since his passing. He allowed me to unleash all of my suppressed emotions for what seemed like twenty minutes then he held me again until my tears ceased and my breathing returned to normal.

"I know about all of this." I looked at him quizzically, but a part of me believed him. He continued, "You're not alone. I have always been closer than you think. You have given up on life a long time ago which blinded you from seeing me. It does no good staying here when it is not your time. Your body will only be stuck in this space until you are ready to move on. You have to go back."

"But I don't know how. I can't live life the same without you," my voice quivered as I held back the rush of tears fighting its way to release.

"You cannot leave our son behind without a father nor his mother." He placed his hand on my cheek. "I have known about our baby since before my passing. I was only waiting for your big, dramatic surprise." He winked at me and placed his lips on my cheek. "I know you are angry because of my death and I wish I could heal the pain that it has caused you, but your anger is blocking you from loving our son. Our son is a part of me. The longer you are here in this space, the longer he is gone and he may not be able to return. I have given him half of my heart and I hold the other half here for you if you are ready. With this, you two will never be alone. Don't miss your chance at the future by being stuck in the past."

His words resonated with me as I thought of our time apart. It has been the most agonizing of times, but I have always felt somewhere deep inside that I was still connected to him. As I held on to this hope, the memories that were once fading away from me were beginning to return again.

"You are ready," he nodded with a pleased smile.

"I love you," I whispered to him.

"I love you," he whispered back to me.

The light turned to darkness again in one quick shift and the feeling of stillness returned.

# My Intuition

They say that a woman's intuition is a powerful thing.

It can be strong and clear or come and go quickly like a fling.

With you I had a feeling that you weren't good for my life,

Your constant negative energy slicing through me like a knife

My intuition didn't tell me all at once,

But since I have noticed, I've had to bounce.

Self-doubt, mistrust and anger was all that I felt.

It led me to a place of despair with the hand that you dealt.

My intuition tried to warn me quite a while ago,

But I was naive and still showed up to your show,

While deep down my stomach burned with discomfort,

# This Stage of Life - Self Discovery

And my mind is telling me to leave, run away, abort!

Now that I have gone, I feel so relieved.

God showed me your ways and told me to leave.

I don't blame you, being with you was a lesson learned.

I still miss you, yes my heart continues to burn.

I hope I taught you as much as you have taught me,

And one day we'll both be loved, happy and free.

I wish you the best as we move on to the next,

And to my intuition, I thank you.

# Bad Days

Not every day will be full of laughter and peace.

Emotions are a dynamic factor that cannot always be controlled.

Old habits await in the shadows for these days.

Just the slightest negativity will awaken them,

And when they attack, they come in full force,

Bringing old memories, bad energy and despair,

To bring you down with them to walk the path you have already been through.

Misery feels best when it has company.

It will tear you down to the point of no return,

But you know better than to go this way.

Calm your mind, lead with your heart, walk before you run and bring positivity from above.

You have what you need within you to get through these bad days.

Soon these days will become brief moments.

Take your time and breathe.

I will see you on the other side.

# Affirmations

Do you know how powerful words can be?

What you say can become what you see.

Your whispers and thoughts are not safe.

If you believe it, it will come to place.

I once was living an empty life full of stress and unhappiness,

Every day worse than the last, pushing myself until I collapsed in stillness.

The words from my mind were loud and clear.

I was weak.

I was unloved.

I was alone.

The bed sunk deeper until I could get out of it no more.

# This Stage of Life - Self Discovery

Trying to find my will to fight just made me sore.

I ran away from my troubles to the one place I felt safe.

It took me four weeks to get out of bed and meet my troubles face to face.

One step at a time I pulled myself higher,

Leaving everything behind that did not meet my desire.

I learned to calm my negative mind,

And fill it with all of the positivity I could find.

Now I speak from the heart.

I am strong.

I am loved.

I am in good company.

Intent is important to the value of words.

"I say what I mean and mean what I say."

You can be your own worst enemy when words come into play.

Be kind and have faith in your beliefs.

Focus on your dreams and you will be saved many griefs.

# Reality Hits Hard

Damn.

I never knew life would be like this.

I moved out into the big bad world with my head held high.

I had all different plans and expectations for how my life would go.

I get it now when they say: Expectation vs Reality.

I have not had one thing in my life go according to plan.

I wanted to be a doctor in a hospital,

But who knew that healthcare was such a toxic place?

The long hours and stress were not worth the pay.

I wanted to live in a high-rise apartment straight out of college,

But who knew that everything was so expensive in life?

# This Stage of Life - Self Discovery

Rent, Gas, Utilities, Food, Healthcare, Insurance, Clothes, the list goes on.

I thought the world would be kind to me.

I gave so much of myself to others while holding an empty palm up in return.

I am grateful for God's plan and the path he put me on but...

Damn.

I faced my reality after I was left to live on my own.

I look back at myself as a naive little fool.

All of the expectations I had only set me back.

It took a year to accept my fate and give up the control I thought I had.

I had many dark days full of tears as I hid under the covers.

I fought reality for so long.

But who knew reality hits this hard?

It took me a while to realize that the person I was fighting was myself,

Wasting my time, telling myself to like something I clearly disliked,

Telling myself that this is how it is supposed to be,

Just stick to the plan.

I was okay with hurting myself trying to be who I am not.

I finally put down my gloves.

There was no way I could win this fight.

I opened my arms instead,

To embrace reality and thank God every day.

I enjoy my new reality now,

The one I make for myself every day.

# ...But

One day I want to...but, I don't know.

I think I should...but maybe not.

That would be amazing...but I can't.

I feel like...but I may be wrong.

I want to go...but not anytime soon.


Please, just stop.

Deep down you know what you want.

Life is too short to be unsure.

Take as many experiences as you can.

Live for yourself and live for today.

# Spoiled, Not Rotten

Some may say that I am spoiled.

For a long time, I would disagree.

The word seemed so degrading and insulting.

I would be so offended and fight to prove them wrong,

But why?

If I am spoiled because my parents gave me their all and more,

Or because I am an only child,

Or even if I am given unconditional love no matter my mistakes,

Then fine, call me spoiled.

But remember, there is a difference between spoiled and spoiled rotten,

And I know for sure I am not spoiled rotten.

# This Stage of Life - Self Discovery

While I am receiving in bounties, I am also learning the act of giving.

While I am given unconditional love, I am also learning the value of loving myself for who I am.

While I am blessed financially, I am also learning the value of money.

I was taught that others are not as fortunate and to always be grateful for what I have.

I was taught to work for my own and depend on no one.

So yes, maybe my parents did spoil me,

But I would never say that all they did was "too much,"

Because they raised a daughter full of love in a world full of hate,

A daughter who worked three jobs in her undergraduate to support them supporting me,

A daughter who gives back to her community and church whenever she can,

A daughter with two degrees, four certifications and published books,

A daughter who values true healthy love over random flings.

I may be full of myself and full of attitude,

But I know what I deserve.

This head on my shoulders is strong, wise and always held high,

So call me spoiled if you want,

But know I was spoiled to be great, not to be rotten.

# Gorgeous

Your hair,

Gorgeous.

Your skin,

Gorgeous.

Your body,

Gorgeous.

Your style,

Gorgeous.

Your smile,

Gorgeous.

Your heart,

Gorgeous.

Your mind,

Gorgeous.

Your soul,

Gorgeous.

All that you are is gorgeous.

No one can be the person you are.

Even though you may not feel gorgeous every day,

Your beauty shines from within.

Know that even on your worst days,

Your crown gleams in the light.

King or Queen, hold your head high.

This world is already yours,

And what is yours will never make you bow down.

Understand your worth is greater than you believe.

Whether you believe in my God or live life as you please,

As long as you are positive you are able to achieve,

But change does not come from just speaking your desires.

Believe in your faith and bring your words to action.

# This Stage of Life - Self Discovery

All jokes aside, it is time to focus on yourself.

Believe, trust and love,

It all begins with you.

Right your wrongs and live in the present,

For all that you do in this moment,

Will guide you onto the next moment.

God exists and so does the Devil.

All the good you do will be followed by more good,

And all the bad you do will be followed by more bad.

Trust in yourself enough to be the person you want to be.

You are gorgeous to all the eyes that can see,

Including the most important eyes belonging to you.

# *Slacking*

Tell me, why is it so easy to take a break from your grind?

Telling yourself that you will just take a little time off and come back stronger.

Yeah, right.

One day turns into two, then, three or maybe even four.

You may go back to your grind for one day in-between.

Half of your heart is with you and half is longing to be somewhere else.

Then you make up an excuse to not come back the next day.

You end your week as a slacker with half-made promises you will not fulfill.

With a shrug, your grind goes to the back of your mind,

# This Stage of Life - Self Discovery

But no one is there to punish you so it must all be okay.

I mean…it is your grind, your side hustle, your dream.

The only person losing from your slacking is you,

But we are all human and deserve a break.

A break: a pause, a rest, with intent to return.

This is not to those who take their time to build their grind,

Coming and going with better ideas than the last.

This is to those who limit their minds to being all or nothing,

Those who give up too easily on their journey to greatness.

This is about consistency; being on it every day at every hour,

But that word brings too much pressure and a standard to live up to.

Nothing in our daily lives stays consistent to the day prior no matter how hard we try.

Do not allow your dream to turn into a chore.

Stay passionate, true and strong.

Frequency is greater than consistency.

The more you work on your grind the better it will grow.

It all depends on you.

# Boundaries

My boundaries are not walls waiting to be broken,

By some 'special' person willing to cross the limits and test my patience.

It took me years to build these boundaries for myself,

Brick by brick I built through the pain, the tears and the joy.

These boundaries make me stand out in a crowd.

They set me apart from the secure and the insecure.

I love and honor my boundaries for showing me what I deserve.

So, while I may accept your apology after your blatant disrespect,

You are no longer welcome to be a part of my life,

Just so you can tear me down again in the future by removing a piece of me.

## This Stage of Life - Self Discovery

This love I have for myself is greater than any pain.

Build those walls and never settle for less.

# *My Songbird* IV

It is the second night in almost two weeks that I have been able to sleep at home in my own bed, but I cannot stay asleep no matter how hard I try. Outside of my bedroom door I hear the familiar cry and I cover my head with the nearby pillow. I stay hidden beneath the pillow until I hear the guest bedroom door open, the shuffle of my mom's bedroom slippers to open another room's door and then silence. I wait a few moments to enjoy the silence then I roll onto my favorite side of the bed, your side, to drift off to sleep.

About two hours later I am awoken again by the familiar cry. This time I grab two pillows to cover each ear as I stare at the ceiling waiting for the cries to stop. I watch the ceiling fan spin slowly above me. Hypnotized I think back to the day he was born, the day my world had stopped, literally.

They told me that my heart stopped once and his heart stopped twice. I believe our first death was in remembrance of you and his second death was in remembrance of me. When they brought us back to life we were kept apart for "observation" as they say. I cried and pleaded for my baby for two days before I was able to see him. He was locked in a clear bin connected to tubes and wires and I was locked on bed rest unable to walk to him. I was shown pictures, videos and medical facts proving that he was getting stronger, but nothing filled the hole of holding my first-born baby in my hands.

On the third day, they pushed me in a wheelchair to see my baby for the first time. We were still kept apart by the glass partition between us. The oxygen mask covered his face and his eyes were closed. Without getting a good look at each other, I was wheeled back to my prison.

On the fourth day the tears had stopped.

On the fifth day everything happened at once. He was strong enough now which meant skin-to-skin contact, breastfeeding and therapy of all kinds. The first time I held him I saw your face, we locked eyes and a tear rolled down my cheek. For a second, I felt peace and happiness, but it was short-lived. The tears began almost immediately after he was in my arms. His screams made it impossible to breastfeed though I was constantly encouraged to do so. We had missed our opportunity to bond and he did not know me. My heart was broken.

We were kept in the hospital for three more days, still unable to form a bond. Then three more days we stayed with my former, soon-to-be in-laws. Now, I am home with my mother in the guest room and I know it is because none of them believe I am able to do this on my own and I believe them.

"You don't hear him crying?" My mother stormed into my room holding the wailing baby in her arms. I had learned to tune out the sound of his cries since we left the hospital. She looked exhausted, her hair was disheveled, her eyes swollen and red. My head was still surrounded by pillows which she widened her eyes at. "Are you ignoring him?" The sound of disbelief was apparent in

63

her voice as she screamed at me over the screams of the baby.

"No!" I scream back.

"This is your baby. You have to take care of him. We can't keep helping you if you don't help yourself." She swayed left to right trying to soothe the baby with her body.

I roll over and cover my entire body, from head-to-toe, with my blanket. "I am taking care of him," I muttered.

She scoffed and ripped the covers off of me. "They told me that you didn't get out of bed once to feed or change him." She mentioned my in-laws. "You made them do everything for him for three days and now you're doing the same with me. I accepted it for the first night, but this is not going on any longer." She gently placed the baby on the left side of the bed and started heading for the door.

"Wait, mom!" I sit upright in the bed. "What am I supposed to do with him?"

She shook her head and sighed, "Feed him, change him, love him. Do what you feel is best to care for him. He's yours. I'm leaving this afternoon." Then she closed the door, leaving me alone with a crying baby that I barely knew. I watched him cry for a few minutes before taking him in my arms. His diaper is dry so I rule that out as I try to figure out the cause of his tears.

*He must be hungry*, I thought. Fear washed over my body as I remember my multiple failed attempts at breastfeeding. I sigh, releasing the fear and doubt that I have as I free my breast from under my shirt.

Remembering the nurse's instructions, I cradle my son in my hands and lean my chest over him to guide my nipple to his mouth.

64

He ignored my first few attempts and chose to continue wailing with dissatisfaction. I reposition myself on the bed while lifting his head slightly higher. Just as I was about to give up and go retrieve a pre-pumped bottle from the fridge, I felt the latch. My heart skipped a beat as I looked down to him suckling at my breast with his eyes closed. I chuckled in disbelief then a full-blown laugh escaped my mouth at the same time tears began to pour from my eyes.

I was full of emotion that was being forced out of me all because of this seven-pound baby in my arms. My baby. I watched his eyes flutter, his long black eyelashes floating above his eyes like a grateful butterfly. His dark brown eyes stare into mine as we share this moment together. I could feel our bond growing stronger with each drop of milk leaving my body and entering his. My heart feels full as I admire his every feature. His round nose is identical to his father, but his wide brown eyes are from me. I smile as he closes his hand around my finger. He had stopped feeding and was quiet now. The orange-yellow glow of the rising sun engulfed his face. I looked toward the window watching the sunrise when I heard a familiar song. With a flutter of its wings, my once missing songbird returned to its perch outside of my window after almost nine months of being gone.

It sang us a tune as the sun rose in the background then fluttered off in the direction it came from. I looked down at my sleeping baby and pecked a kiss on his forehead. This time, I was not worried about my songbird's departure. I knew that for as long as I loved my son, my songbird would live within me, just like his father.

# *Thank You*

What I have accomplished here are more than just words on paper.

I have finally found a way to understand myself a little deeper.

The joy I have found in releasing my fears,

Helped to free me from a life that I could not bear.

When I started this journey, I was in a dark place.

I had little happiness in my life and I felt like a disgrace.

While things may have seemed great looking in from the outside,

There was something growing inside me that only brought me despair.

I lied so much trying to make it seem like everything was okay.

To the people closest to me all I wanted was that they pray,

But now I found my safe space where I am free from it all.

# This Stage of Life - Self Discovery

I found a way to release my emotions without having a downfall.

I say "Thank you," to all the people I have gained and lost along the way.

I hope that I have given to this life as much as it has taken away.

I feel a new happiness by finding myself.

I learned that loving myself is the greatest wealth.

Thank you to the highest power for giving me the courage to write.

# About the Author

**Jasmine Samuel** was born in Brooklyn, New York and grew up in Virginia where she has made her home. She has always been fascinated with writing and published her first book at the age of thirteen. Being an only child, she has always strived to stay busy and entertained as she has dabbled in numerous creative outlets such as competitive dance, piano and flute, sports, and traveling. She is taking her time to enjoy her youth and loves adventure and trying new things. Her favorite hobby is eating at new restaurants and judging their food like a professional chef. Jasmine enjoys education and learning new things as she is working on her Master's degree and plans to pursue her PhD in the future. "This Stage of Life" is Jasmine Samuel's first self-published book.